The Sunken Living Room

by

David Caudle

FOUNDED 1830

NEW YORK HOLLYWOOD LONDON TORONTO

SAMUELFRENCH.COM

ISBN 978-0-573-66249-2   Printed in U.S.A.   #20868

IMPORTANT BILLING AND CREDIT REQUIREMENTS

All producers of *THE SUNKEN LIVING ROOM* *must* give credit to the Author of the Play in all programs distributed in connection with performances of the Play, and in all instances in which the title of the Play appears for the purposes of advertising, publicizing or otherwise exploiting the Play and/or a production. The name of the Author *must* appear on a separate line on which no other name appears, immediately following the title and *must* appear in size of type not less than fifty percent of the size of the title type.

THE SUNKEN LIVING ROOM by David Caudle was first presented at the New Theatre in Coral Gables, Florida, on September 27, 2006 as a co-production with Southern Rep in New Orleans. Directed by Ryan Rilette, Artistic Director of Southern Rep; Set Design by Jesse Dreikosen; Costume Design by K. Blair Brown; Lighting by Michael Foster; Sound Design by Ricardo Mungaray; Stage Manager Arienne Pelletier.

WADE	John Magaro
LYNNETTE	Pamela Roza
CHIP	Rudy Mungaray
TAMMY	Arienne Ellison

The Co-Production re-opened at Southern Rep in New Orleans on January 17, 2007. Directed Ryan Rilette; Set Design by Jesse Dreikosen; Costume Design by Rayna Middleton; Lighting Design by Martin L. Sachs; Sound Design by Ricardo Mungaray; Stage Manager, Desiree Stevenson.

WADE	John Magaro
LYNNETTE	Staci Robbins
CHIP	Rudy Mungaray
TAMMY	Arienne Ellison

THE SUNKEN LIVING ROOM was originally slotted for a World Premiere at Southern Rep in November of 2005. The production was cast and ready to begin rehearsals when Hurricane Katrina struck. The author wishes to thank and acknowledge Rafael De Acha, then-Artistic Director of New Theatre, and Ricky J. Martinez, current Artistic Director of New Theatre for offering the displaced production a home. The author would also like to acknowledge the original actors cast locally in New Orleans, who were prevented from playing the roles they had auditioned for and won.

LYNNETTE	Stacy Arton
CHIP	Nick Gomez
TAMMY	Mary Cobb

THE SUNKEN LIVING ROOM was developed in part in the Downstage Miami Playwriting Workshop organized by Rem Cabrera of the Dade County Department of Cultural Affairs.

CHARACTERS

(in order of appearance)

LYNNETTE, 40s. The attention-starved wife of an air line pilot.

WADE, 16. Lynnette's youngest son. Slender, effeminate, naive. A bookworm.

CHIP, 17. Wade's older brother. Sexy, athletic, emotionally volatile.

TAMMY, 17. Chip's sexually-experienced pothead girlfriend.

SETTING

The sunken living room of a suburban Miami home. November, 1978.

ACT ONE

Scene One

(Miami, Florida. Around dusk, early November, 1978. Lights up on the sunken living room of a suburban middle-class home. The front door opens onto a tiled foyer containing a small table, a mirror and a cuckoo clock. A hallway leads to the bedrooms offstage. A railing flanks the foyer, then turns along the back edge of the two steps down into the living room proper. The steps and the living room floor are carpeted with a plush shag. An entertainment unit stands in a corner, filled with record albums, a stereo, and posed photos of the family and its individual members. Opposite the foyer, two steps lead back up to the main floor level under an archway leading to the formal dining room, kitchen and master bedroom. How much of the dining room is visible onstage can vary, but its looming presence should be felt, even more formal and less frequented than this museum of a living room. At lights up, the room is deadly still except for the ticking of the cuckoo clock. **LYNNETTE** *enters through the dining room archway. She is in her early forties, quite attractive and stylish but somehow distracted. Her son,* **WADE,** *16, follows eagerly behind her. Bookish and rather effeminate, he is barefoot, in shorts and a t-shirt.)*

WADE. Mom, wait! Turn around a minute.

LYNNETTE. What? I want to get going.

WADE. One of your eyebrows is like, missing.

LYNNETTE. Are you kidding me?

(Lynnette stops at the mirror in the foyer.)

Oh. Christ.

(She sets her purse on the little table and fishes in it.)

Son of a … will you go get me my eyebrow pencil?

WADE. Jawohl, Herr Kommandant!

(She begins other touch-ups to her make-up.)

LYNNETTE. I might have dropped it somewhere in the master bedroom.

WADE. I've been sent to the Rrrussian Frrront!

LYNNETTE. *(to herself)* That's one way to describe it.

WADE. On Hogan's Heroes the other day, there was this –

LYNNETTE. Will you go get the pencil? I don't want to hear about Hogan's Heroes. I don't know how anybody can laugh about war. You watch entirely too much TV.

(beat)

Listen to me. I say one thing and the whole repertoire comes spilling out. No more TV. Eat your vegetables. You'll go blind.

(realizing the sensitive allusion)

…Oh…

*(**CHIP** enters from the hall. He's 17, charismatic and rock star sexy. Though only a year older than Wade, he is physically much more developed.*

He wears bell-bottom jeans and no shirt, and vigorously takes a towel to his wet, shoulder-length hair.)

CHIP. Even if he did go blind, he'd still find it.

*(**LYNNETTE** laughs in spite of herself. Turning bright red, **WADE** exits through the dining room.)*

LYNNETTE. Going somewhere?

CHIP. I'm gonna go pick up Tammy and we're gonna see a movie or something. So…

LYNNETTE. No.

CHIP. Just, like, thirty bucks. I need to get gas, and we might want to grab McDonalds after.

LYNNETTE. Shouldn't twenty be enough?

CHIP. C'mon, mom. Don't you know what gas costs now? Plus, I need a quart of oil and some washer fluid.

LYNNETTE. Have you been neglecting that car?

CHIP. No. That's what I'm *not* doin. That's why I need the bread.

LYNNETTE. I hope you'll go to the filling station before you pick up Tammy. Unless you want to dazzle her with your automotive maintenance skills. Not that she's the particular type, wisely for her.

CHIP. She's not like you, if that's what you mean. But hey, I gave up tryin to find a gal – how does that old song go? Like the gal that dear old dad – that caved to dear old dad, or somethin.

LYNNETTE. Don't try to sweet-talk me, boy. I'm onto your tricks. I'll give you twenty dollars and not a penny more.

CHIP. Mom, please believe me. Thirty bucks is barely enough these days.

LYNNETTE. Well... Let me see your eyes.

CHIP. Aw, c'mon, mom. I ain't doin' that sh – stuff anymore.

LYNNETTE. You better not be. How come the yard's not mowed?

CHIP. Duh! It rained. The grass is wet.

LYNNETTE. When the grass is mowed, you can have thirty bucks. Your father told me not to give you a penny until it was done.

CHIP. That's not fair! I couldn't stop the goddamn rain!

LYNNETTE. Keep talking like that, Mister, and you'll be grounded.

CHIP. Oh, like you don't cuss?

LYNNETTE. Wade! Where are you with that pencil?

CHIP. Maybe he ducked into the bathroom for a quickie.

LYNNETTE. Stop!

CHIP. C'mon, mama. Yo, hot mama, lookin' fine, just slide me thirty and I'll stay in line.

LYNNETTE. *(succumbing to his charms)* Alright, but you have to get that yard done tomorrow. Your father will be home the day after, and if it's not done, he'll crap a cupcake.

(She hands him the bills.

CHIP *slaps her a high five, and exits back down the hallway.)*

LYNNETTE *(cont.) (calling after him)* When your father calls at nine, you better be here! You and Tammy can go to McDonald's after that, if need be. Chip? Did you hear me?

(WADE returns with an eyebrow pencil. She goes to work at the mirror.)

Great. Thanks, honey.

WADE. Where's *he* going?

LYNNETTE. To the movies with Tammy.

WADE. Is she back?

LYNNETTE. From where?

WADE. I thought she moved to Massachusetts with her mom.

LYNNETTE. Moved? No, you must be mistaken.

WADE. She probably wanted to get as far away from him as possible.

LYNNETTE. If she moved to Massachusetts, how could he be going to the movies with her?

WADE. Exactly my point. He's such a stupid, lying, stupid jerk.

LYNNETTE. That's enough of that. Your brother is not stupid.

WADE. What college did he get into? Or is he waiting to see if he actually *graduates*?

LYNNETTE. Not everybody is a scholar. It doesn't mean he's stupid. You need to stop saying that.

WADE. Oh, I can't say he's stupid, which he is, but it's okay for him to give me a hard time about every other single thing on earth?

LYNNETTE. You need to develop a thicker skin, my boy.

WADE. What about *his* skin? He's doing 'ludes again.

LYNNETTE. He says he's not.

WADE. C'mon, mom. Some other stuff, too. He's on something right now, I think.

LYNNETTE. Wade, just mind your own business. Your tattling is not attractive.

WADE. I'm not trying to be attractive. He's just… lying to everybody. How can you think he's telling the truth? How can you let him drive? Give him money?

LYNNETTE. I don't want to hear one more fucking word, pardon my French!

(beat)

Your father and I are satisfied that he's learned his lesson. The car is still drive-able. It's not your concern.

(beat)

How do I look now? Am I not byooootiful?

WADE. Yes…

(She smiles.)

…you are not byooootiful.

*(**LYNNETTE** slaps his arm with mock annoyance.*

Suddenly, the cuckoo clock comes to life. The little door opens and the bird pops out on his perch, cuckooing six times.)

LYNNETTE. You heard the bird. I'll see you later.

*(She heads for the door. **WADE** tags along, pulling on her purse strap.)*

WADE. Oh, I forgot to tell you what I said in French class today. It was really funny. This girl Nina, she –

LYNNETTE. Wade, quit! How will I ever get to be a Life Master if you don't let me out of the house?

WADE. Why do they call it Life Master? Why not just, Bridge Master? Don't they think there's more to life than Bridge? I mean, what if your life sucks? Who wants to be Master of a sucky life?

LYNNETTE. I don't have time to discuss this now, and I don't like your language. Goodbye. Do your homework.

WADE. I got an A on my history paper.

(Beat; **LYNNETTE** *casts him a look of sincere disappointment.)*

LYNNETTE. *(gently admonishing)* You always get an A, and you always brag. It's really not very attractive.

*(***LYNNETTE** *exits.*

WADE *hangs in the open doorway, watching until the car is heard pulling away.*

He closes the front door. Starts toward the hallway, but thinks better of it, to avoid Chip. He turns on the radio, and exits into the dining room. A DJ's voice fills the empty room.)

DJ (V.O.) That was Peter Frampton sayin' "Show me the way," baby. But if you ask me, he could show us the way – to get all those foxy mamas. Shazam! So, for all you hot mamas and Frampton disciples out there who just joined us... You are listening to the new sound of Y-100, bringing South Florida the best of the best new tunes. And, we got the fewest commercial interruptions. But let's face it. The commercials gotta come sometime, right? And looks like that time is... now. A super tune from Supertramp, some Average White Band and some Kansas comin' at ya after a few words from –

CHIP (O.S., *simultaneous with Radio* **DJ)** ....Hey!.... Wade! .... Turn that down!... I'm listenin to 96-X!...... Wade?

*(***WADE** *hurries in with a bowl of Froot Loops. Turns off the radio.*

CHIP *appears in the hallway, half-dressed.)*

CHIP *(cont.)* Did you hear me?

WADE. Sorry. I didn't know how loud it was.

CHIP. You don't have to turn it off. Just turn it down or put it on 96-X.

(CHIP exits.

WADE *pulls an album out of the stack and puts it on the turntable to play. An instrumental song starts, slow and folksy.)*

CHIP (O.S.) *(cont.)* What the hell is that?

(WADE plugs in head phones, so the music is no longer audible to the audience. He puts the head phones on, sits on the floor in front of the stereo and eats, reading lyrics from the album sleeve.

CHIP *enters, now fully dressed, ultra-cool and totally hot. He looks at the album on the stereo, yanks the head phones out, and turns the radio on.*

He turns the knob and finds a hard-rocking instrumental. Cranks it up and plays air guitar.)

WADE. Cut it out!

CHIP. *Cut it out!*

WADE. I was listening to that!

(WADE turns off the radio.)

CHIP. *I was listening to that!* You're such a fairy.

WADE. Shut up!

CHIP. *Shut up!* Ooh, I'm quakin in my boots! Look at you, sittin there eatin your Froot Loops, listenin to that folky shit. You are such a fuckin fairy.

WADE. *(struggling for a snappy comeback)* The situation is reversed!

CHIP. *(laughing) The situation is reversed!* Oooh, burn! You really got me, man. That's a good one. I gotta remember that. *The situation is reversed!*

WADE. You better leave me alone, or I'm gonna tell mom you're lying about Tammy.

CHIP. What the hell are you talkin about?

WADE. I know she went to Massachusetts.

CHIP. Yeah, she fuckin went to Massachusetts, and now she's fuckin back, you fuckin pudwacker.

WADE. She is not! You're the fucking pudwacker!

CHIP. See, that's what separates the cool dudes from the pudwackers. You gotta say fuckin, not fucking. You don't pronounce the 'g.' That takes all the balls out of it. 'slike sayin gosh-darn.

(mockingly effeminate)

Oh, you gosh-darn pudwacker man, you just make me oh so very very mad!

WADE. I don't talk like that.

CHIP. The hell you don't.

*(**WADE** plugs the head phones in and starts the folk album again. He puts on the headphones with defiance.)*

CHIP *(cont.)* Whatever, man. I don't care what you do when I'm not around. Just don't break your arm jerkin off.

*(**CHIP** heads for the door, but stops. He goes back to **WADE**. Grabs the album sleeve and calmly reads some of the lyrics.)*

CHIP *(cont.) (loudly, so Wade can hear through the headphones)* It's pretty cool, I guess. The chick knows how to rhyme.

WADE. This was Allison's record. Not that you care.

CHIP. What do you mean? She's my sister too. Look, you're not really mad at me are you? C'mon. Take those things off. You know I was just kiddin ya. Just tryin to get you toughened up for the big bad world.

WADE. So far, you're the worst part of it, so what's the point?

CHIP. Look, I ain't on the debate squad. I can't talk things around in circles like you can. I've just got common sense, which is what you need in life. What *you* don't have.

*(**WADE** starts to take off the headphones, but won't give Chip that satisfaction.)*

WADE. Dad said that *one time*. That you can be book smart without having common sense. I was there. I heard him. He didn't mean everyone who's book smart has no common sense, and everyone who's *not* book smart *does* have common sense. I have common sense, Chip. And book smarts. You don't have either one.

CHIP. Alright, then. You're so smart, you tell me what to do. I got a big problem, man. Come on.

(**WADE** *slowly takes off the headphones and stops the record.*)

CHIP *(cont.)* It's Tammy. I knocked her up.

WADE. She's pregnant?

CHIP. No, she's fuckin European, what do you think? Yes, she's fuckin pregnant.

WADE. Wow.

CHIP. So? What should I do?

WADE. Are you gonna marry her?

CHIP. How can I marry her? What kinda common sense is that? I'm seventeen years old, man. So is she.

WADE. Are you sure she's not staying in Massachusetts?

CHIP. She ain't stayin in no Massachussetts. I don't know where you get this shit. She's here in Miami right now, knocked up. Jesus! What should we do?

WADE. Well, I guess she could put the baby up for adoption.

CHIP. Adoption? She can't have this baby, man.

WADE. An abortion?

CHIP. So, you're sayin she should get an abortion?

WADE. Well, is that what you meant?

CHIP. I don't know, I'm askin you.

WADE. Maybe you better tell mom.

CHIP. She'll tell dad. You want me to get killed?

WADE. Dad wouldn't –

CHIP. Look what happened to Allison, man. We can't even fuckin say her name anymore. You wish it was me instead of her, don't you?

WADE. It would never be you.

CHIP. You'll see. If dad finds out about this, you'll be the only one left standin. 'Sprobly what you want anyway.

WADE. When school lets out this summer, I'm gonna go find her. I'm gonna pay my own way. I don't care what dad says.

CHIP. How much money you got now?

WADE. I don't know, exactly.

CHIP. 'Cuz I think you're right. I think an abortion is the only way. Thanks, man.

WADE. I didn't say –

CHIP. But if I ask mom and dad for the money, they'll figure it out. You gotta help me, man.

WADE. Chip, I can't give you any money.

CHIP. You got to. I need it, little bro. You gotta help me.

WADE. Get your own job.

CHIP. I can't work at fuckin Burger King, man. Wearin those dorky polyester uniforms and those pussy paper hats.

WADE. Good. I don't want you working with me anyway. But you could work at a gas station or something. Would that be cool enough for you? Paula Doogan's dad owns a gas station, and she's, like, a cool girl. A lot of people think she's pretty and, like, stacked, and stuff.

CHIP. I got to third base with her once. Maybe I could talk to her. Get her to ask her dad.

WADE. Sounds good.

CHIP. Yeah, but I gotta have the money now. Now that you've brought up the abortion thing, you know, that kind of thing is supposed to happen early, or it could be dangerous for Tammy. By the time I start workin and get paid, it might be too late. Why don't you just front me the money now, and I'll pay you back with my first paycheck. Yeah, that's what we better do.

WADE. You don't even have this job yet. How do I know you're gonna even get one?

CHIP. Alright, man. You don't want to help out your only brother, that's cool. What about Tammy? She's gonna be in huge trouble. It could ruin her life.

WADE. I didn't say I wouldn't help. I just... don't know... Besides, my money's all in the bank, and the banks are closed. So for tonight, you just have to forget it.

CHIP. Put a man on the moon, but they can't keep a bank open at night? You don't have any cash on you?

WADE. No. Tammy couldn't get ... an abortion tonight anyway.

CHIP. Yeah, but we'd be ready in the morning. Come on, man. I know you must have a stash here somewhere. Are you gonna help me out, or are you gonna be a pudwacker?

WADE. You just want drug money, is what you want. Tammy's in Massachusetts.

CHIP. That's great. That's just great. I love you, too.

(**CHIP** *storms out, slamming the front door behind him. Lights fade.*)

Scene Two

(An hour or so later. It is now totally dark outside. **WADE** *sits on the living room carpet, using the coffee table as a desk. He reads E.M. Forster's* A Passage to India *and takes notes in a spiral pad. The door flies open.* **TAMMY,** *17, enters, as if pushed. She grabs the railing and stumbles down the two steps, into the living room. Her jeans and halter top hug a terrific bod, offset by unconventional features and scraggly, unflattering hair.* **CHIP** *enters behind her.)*

CHIP. Do you know who this is, douchebag?

WADE. Hi Tammy.

CHIP. Are we in Massachusetts here?

WADE. I'm sorry. I thought you moved there.

CHIP. Is this Massachusetts, or Miami?

WADE. It's Miami.

CHIP. Alright, then. Tammy, go wait in the car.

TAMMY. God.

*(***TAMMY*** exits.)*

CHIP. See?

WADE. Yes, I see. I'm sorry.

CHIP. So, you gonna help me out? Help her out? I got nobody else I can ask.

WADE. Alright, Chip. I will. I'll help you.

CHIP. Thanks, man. I heard it costs, like, two hundred and fifty. You got that much?

WADE. I can get it for you tomorrow.

CHIP. Aw, c'mon, man. You know she's here. I proved it.

WADE. I know. I believe you. But I still don't have any money here. I'll get it for you tomorrow. I promise.

(Beat; Chip is stymied.)

CHIP. Fine!

*(***CHIP*** exits. Wade hears Chip and Tammy argue outside.*

He peers out the window but can't make out their words.
The voices come closer. **WADE** *quickly takes up his book.*
CHIP *and* **TAMMY** *enter.)*

CHIP. Go wait in the room.

TAMMY. God.

*(***TAMMY*** *exits down the hall.)*

WADE. What's wrong?

CHIP. She's not feeling good.

WADE. Morning sickness?

CHIP. Or evening, whatever. I gotta go get her some medicine. It's pretty expensive, though.

WADE. Didn't mom give you any money?

CHIP. Yeah, but I used most of it for the car. Don't you have *anything* in your wallet?

*(***WADE*** *heads for the hallway.)*

Where you goin?

WADE. It's in my Burger King pants.

CHIP. I'll bring 'em out here. Tammy might be…

*(***CHIP*** *exits down the hall and reappears with a pair of dark brown polyester slacks.* **WADE** *fishes his wallet out. Removes a few bills.)*

WADE. Twenty-two. That's all I have. It should be more than enough.

CHIP. I don't know, I hope so. I'll be back.

WADE. Should I do anything?

CHIP. No. No, you just stay out here. She's totally wrecked right now.

WADE. I hate to think of her back there alone, all miserable.

CHIP. She's better off by herself. Remember when Scheherazade got leukemia? She stopped eating, and she was always hiding, and wouldn't let anybody pick her up or pet her or anything? That's how Tammy feels. The best thing you can do is just leave her totally alone. But, whatever you do, don't mention anything about what I told you. You gotta promise me that.

WADE. What if she brings it up?

CHIP. That ain't gonna happen. Promise me.

WADE. Okay. I promise. I wouldn't know how to talk about that anyway.

CHIP. You're alright, you know that?

WADE. Gee, I wasn't sure. What a relief.

CHIP. I'm being serious, man.

WADE. I know. And Chip?

CHIP. Yeah?

WADE. I'm kinda glad. Not that this is happening, but. You know. That you... we... you know...

CHIP. I know. Me, too.

> (**CHIP** exits. His car is heard peeling out.
>
> **WADE** stares down the hallway for a long time, and finally goes back to his book.
>
> Soon, **TAMMY** enters from the hallway and lingers in the foyer.)

TAMMY. You think I could have something to drink?

WADE. (in awe of her pregnancy) Sure. So... how are you? You can sit out here if you want.

TAMMY. Nah. If you could get me a Tab or something, I'll just go wait in you guys's room.

WADE. No problem. Just sit down a minute. Go on. Sit.

> (Beat; she hesitates.)

TAMMY. Chip said this room is, like, off limits except for fancy guests.

WADE. Well, we never have any.

TAMMY. It just looks so... clean.

WADE. That's because nobody ever sits on this couch. Nobody ever uses this room. Except to walk through, or turn on the stereo. When it's just me at home I like to give this room something to do. I think of it as my room. I don't like to do anything in mine and Chip's room but sleep. It's impossible to study in there. I mean, he's always –

TAMMY. I can't believe you guys still share a room at this age. What's that office back there for?

WADE. It's my dad's.

TAMMY. But what does a pilot need an office for?

WADE. To study. The airplane manuals are like phone books, they're so thick. He has them for DC-8s, 9s,10s, and 727s, 737s, 747s, and I don't know what all. Every once in a while he has to take a test.

TAMMY. Even though he already has the job? That sucks.

WADE. He gets a lot of headaches. Didn't Chip tell you this?

TAMMY. He told me that was your sister's room before, right?

WADE. Yep.

TAMMY. They should give it to you or Chip.

WADE. That's okay. This is my room, like I said. By default, as it were. Except when I'm sleeping. Go on. Sit down.

(She goes into the living room but doesn't sit.)

WADE *(cont.) (glancing at her midsection)* You don't *look...* tired.

TAMMY. That's 'cuz I'm not. Nice stereo. Could I see what you guys have?

WADE. Yeah. We have tons of records. Go on. Check it out. I'll rake the carpet afterward. Nobody'll ever know.

TAMMY. *(referring to his books)* I'm not keeping you from, like, studying?

WADE. There are headphones right there. You can use those.

TAMMY. Oh. Okay. Cool.

(She looks through the albums as WADE goes back to his book.)

WADE. I feel bad. I kept saying you were in Massachusetts.

TAMMY. I was. But just for a couple of weeks. I can't believe it's still this hot down here.

WADE. I know. I'm hoping for a cold front, but they usually don't get down this far until December. Hey, was it snowing in Massachusetts?

TAMMY. No, but it was pretty cold. There were no leaves on the trees.

WADE. Wow. I've never seen snow, in real life, I mean. Have you?

TAMMY. Yeah, it's okay. I wouldn't mind eating a handful of it right about now. Listen, do you want me to go get that drink myself?

WADE. Oh, man. I'm sorry. I'm such a space cadet. I'll be right back.

(**WADE** *runs out, and shortly re-enters.*)

WADE *(cont.)* My mom drank all the Tab. Is Seven-Up okay? Or do you think milk would be… better?

TAMMY. Milk? I said I was *thirsty.*

WADE. Oh, right. So… Seven-Up, then? Seven-Up. Coming right, well, Up.

(*With a chuckle,* **WADE** *rushes off through the dining room.*

TAMMY *pulls a pack of cigarettes and a lighter out of her pocket, lights a cigarette.*

WADE *returns with two tall glasses of Seven-Up with ice.* **TAMMY** *takes hers without ceremony.*)

TAMMY. It's okay if I smoke, right? There's this gargantuan ashtray here, so I figured…

WADE. *(it's not really okay)* Yeah, it's okay. My mom smokes all the time. Just, not usually in here. Just… be careful with the ashes, okay?

TAMMY. Want one?

WADE. No, thanks. I don't smoke. You… didn't find anything you wanted to listen to?

TAMMY. Nah, not right now.

WADE. Oh… okay…

(He starts toward his book. **TAMMY** *picks it up first. Reads the synopsis on the back.)*

TAMMY. *(gesturing to the book)* So… who's Mrs. Moore?

WADE. Oh. She's an English lady who goes to India and dies.

TAMMY. How does she die?

WADE. Heart attack, I guess. She's actually on a boat on her way home, but doesn't make it. People say her name a lot. They just keep repeating her name over and over, "Mrs. Moore, Mrs. Moore…"

TAMMY. What, was she, like Farrah Fawcett or something?

WADE. No, she was old, but people just really liked her. This Indian wise man said she had an "old soul."

TAMMY. A lot of good it did her. I like reading about *real* people. Like Isadora Duncan. Know who she was?

WADE. I've heard the name.

TAMMY. She was this amazing dancer in, around, the turn of the century. She was really famous, but she did drugs and had kids without bein married. She was, like, the first hippy. Her life was full of tragedy and she croaked before her time.

WADE. How did she croak?

TAMMY. She used to wear these long flowing scarves, and one time she was in a convertible, because they had cars back then too, and her scarf got caught in the wheel and snapped her neck. Just goes to show.

WADE. What?

TAMMY. I'm not sure, but if *that* doesn't go to show something, I don't know what would.

WADE. See, that's why I like reading novels. ~~You can tell what they go to show.~~ When I start getting it, you know, understanding things, like about people, it's great. It's like I'm learning things I didn't know I knew.

TAMMY. There's only one thing to learn about people. They suck.

WADE. There are plenty of good people. Chip –

TAMMY. Chip just wants a piece. That's all I am to him. A walking twat.

WADE. *(suppressing his shock at her language)* He doesn't know how to admit his feelings. He's kind of spoiled.

TAMMY. What do you mean? Has he said anything to you about me?

WADE. No, it's just, my mom and dad both like him best. They always did. It's so obvious. ~~He's always been used to people liking him. Just because he's~~ – I mean, he's good-looking and good at sports. He knows it feels good to be liked, but he doesn't know it feels even better to like people back.

TAMMY. Sometimes he can be soooo fun. And then he just goes off. For no reason.

WADE. He's just a little volatile sometimes.

TAMMY. What?

WADE. You know, high-strung.

TAMMY. You're so much smarter than he is.

WADE. I'm in all Honors classes.

TAMMY. Wow.

WADE. I have a 3.8 average. The only things that wreck it are P.E. and Driver's Ed. I hit a lot of cones. But I'm in the top five percentile.

TAMMY. That's… amazing. ~~Yeah, I know, you're a brain.~~

WADE. Well, you could be, too.

TAMMY. No, I'm a freak. Because I smoke pot and have sex and skip school. There's one freak in student government, but she's really a brain, who's just a drug addict with mental problems. Mostly freaks don't go in for student government. I think some of the *brains* have sex, too, and drink a little beer sometimes but they're in *a lot* of clubs and student government. The rednecks drink beer and have sex and skip school, but some of *them* are in student government. The *jocks* drink beer, smoke pot and have sex and skip school, but still some of *them* are in student government.

(beat)

That's what Chip is. A freak-jock. If he didn't have black friends he'd be a freak-jock-redneck, 'cuz he's also friends with some of *them*, and I know he's bagged a few of the *brain* chicks, so actually you could say he's a freak-jock-redneck-brain, pretty much just across-the-board kinda guy.

(beat)

Except he's not in student government.

(beat)

~~Me, I'm just a freak.~~ And you're just a brain, right?

~~WADE. I went to a Jefferson Starship concert once.~~

TAMMY. ~~Yeah, but~~... I mean, you don't smoke or drink or skip school or... any of that, do you?

WADE. Not really.

TAMMY. Don't you ever wanna know what it feels like?

WADE. Not really.

TAMMY. I guess that's good in a way, but aren't you supposed to be, like, trying things out, and *testing boundaries*? That's what the guidance counselor says I'm doing. She says it'll be good for me in the long run. But she said I shouldn't tell anyone that she said that.

WADE. Ms. Wilkins?

TAMMY. Don't tell anybody I told you that. I don't want to get her in trouble. She's really cool. I think she smokes weed, actually. Once I thought she was about to offer me some, but the vice principal came in. I actually think she digs me. You know, like "lezzz be friends." It's cool, though.

WADE. I guess I don't know. I don't really go to the guidance counselors.

TAMMY. Well, if you did, she'd be the first to tell you, it's not so good to be all polite and perfect all the time.

WADE. She doesn't know my family. Allison and Ch – well, Allison already got so messed up –

TAMMY. You were gonna say Chip, too, right? It's okay. You can say what you want about him. I won't tell him. Besides, I know better than anybody how fucked up he is. *out loom –*

(She lights another cigarette off the first one, stubbing the butt out in the ashtray.)

WADE. So, don't you see? I'm the only one left. If I get messed up too, my parents'll probably just go crazy.

TAMMY. Do you think so? They don't seem like wimps to me.

WADE. I don't mean they're wimps, I just mean –

TAMMY. I don't think there are *any* wimps in your family.

(beat; flirtatious now)

I know you're kinda gentle and everything, but I bet you're full of surprises when you wanna be.

WADE. *(oblivious to her tone)* Today, in French class, I said the funniest thing to this girl, Nina. She was –

TAMMY. I'm a fox, right? Don't you think I'm a fox? If you saw me walking down the street and didn't know me, wouldn't you say, "Wow, she's a fox?"

WADE. Yeah.

TAMMY. Don't sound so enthusiastic. What? What's wrong with me?

WADE. Nothing.

TAMMY. If you put a bag over my head, right?

WADE. No!

TAMMY. That's what your brother thinks.

WADE. No, I'm sure he doesn't.

TAMMY. Why do you stick up for him? You should hear what he says about you.

WADE. Couldn't be any worse than what he tells me to my face every single stupid day.

TAMMY. Why does he have to be such a great lay? I fuckin hate the guy but he's such a great lay. God, look how red you are. What's the matter? You think I'm a slut, don't you?

WADE. *(collecting his thoughts)* I think you must be really upset.

TAMMY. You wouldn't tell me what you really think anyway.

WADE. Well, I mean, you're always with Chip. It's not really my place, you know? But I guess, now that I'm kinda involved... I mean, you can tell me, you know. If you need to talk about it...

TAMMY. Talk about what?

WADE. Well, I'm not supposed to say...

TAMMY. Oh, my God! He told you?! I'm gonna kill that bastard!

(She slams her cigarette butt in the ashtray and paces the room with furious strides. WADE makes sure the butt is out.)

WADE. Don't worry! I won't tell anyone! Tammy, calm down! I told him I'd help. I will. Whatever you decide to do, I'll help.

TAMMY. Help? How the hell can you help?

WADE. I have money! I work after school. I can do something.

TAMMY. But there's nothing to do now. It's all done already.

WADE. What's done?

TAMMY. I already got rid of it! cut from

(beat; quieter)

Why the hell do you think I went to Massachusetts?

WADE. Does Chip know?

TAMMY. What do you think? So does your friggin father. He's the one who paid for it.

WADE. My father?

TAMMY. Damn right. Your father gave my mom five hundred bucks, and she took me to Massachusetts, to the doctor she used to use.

WADE. Your mom?

TAMMY. Yeah. She went to that doctor four times before she had me and came down here.

(**WADE** *gapes at her, confused and horrified.*)

TAMMY *(cont.)* It happens. What, you don't believe me? Yeah, sometimes you can't have kids after that many, but I'm a miracle baby. I'm gonna find the cure for cancer. What is your problem? Why are you looking at me like that?

WADE. Chip just asked me for money tonight, for … an abortion.

TAMMY. Well, it's not for me. He must have knocked up some other bitch. Or he just wanted some cash to get high.

WADE. He *is* doing drugs, isn't he? I mean, besides pot?

TAMMY. Where do you think he went right now?

WADE. He's such a liar!

TAMMY. Don't tell me you're that gullible? Son of a bitch! Don't you see what he did? He didn't just lie! He used me – our baby – our dead fuckin baby – as an excuse to con you out of money for friggin dope! And you're all, *I can help, I have a job!* I thought you were supposed to be the smart one!

WADE. You wanna talk about smart? I'm not the one who's hanging around with Chip because I *want* to.

TAMMY. *(aggressively)* Well, I'm hanging around with you, now.

WADE. Why? We've never said more than five words to each other before tonight. Why, all of a sudden? You come over. He drops you off and leaves us alone. You're supposed to help him get money from me, aren't you? That's why you spent all this time talking to me. You never did before. What went wrong? He didn't tell you what the story was supposed to be? Anyway, it doesn't matter. I told him I don't keep a stash at home, and that's the truth, so you can just give it up.

TAMMY. We were supposed to go to the movies, to see Seargent Pepper's. Then he brings me here for that stupid Massachusetts moment, and then he tells me he's gonna score some 'ludes. I got mad and told him

I wasn't going. Grass mellows him out. But on 'ludes, he's really cranky. I told him to take me back to my stepdad's house, but he wouldn't, so… I refused to get back in the car.

WADE. Took you awhile to come up with that.

TAMMY. It's true. I just… can't believe you think I'd do something that mean.

WADE. Why should you care what I think?

TAMMY. You're one of the only people I know who has, you know, *room to talk.*

(*The compliment catches* **WADE** *off guard.* **TAMMY** *pulls an album from the shelf.*)

TAMMY *(cont.)* Joni Mitchell? I love her. She's so artistic.

WADE. That's my sister's record.

TAMMY. Do you mind if I play it?

WADE. Kinda.

TAMMY. Oh. Okay. How about this?

(*She holds up Heart's* Dreamboat Annie *album.*)

Magic Man. Crazy on You. These chicks rock, man. I just really feel like I need to rock out with some chicks right now. You know? Can I?

WADE. I'd rather you didn't.

TAMMY. Was that your sister's, too?

WADE. No, but –

TAMMY. Don't tell me you don't like Heart? I mean, I know everybody's entitled to their opinions, but how can anybody not agree about Heart? What? Did your sister not like them? I can't believe a chick wouldn't like Heart.

WADE. I don't wanna talk about Heart!

TAMMY. Okay! Geez.

(*beat*)

You know, I never actually met your sister, like, to talk to, but I saw her around school some. Then she left.

Then she was back. Then she left again, and that was
before I started going with Chip, so there was never
any reason... I know it's considered, like, a family tragedy or something around here. But that's so retarded.
People are starting to shack up all over the place now.
And not just the hippies. It's no big deal anymore. Hel-
luva lot better than bein in the friggin *Moonies.*

WADE. Children of God.

TAMMY. Yeah, right. Children of some creep who makes his
kids beg on the highway so he can have a limo and a
mansion on Star Island. They gave me their pamphlets
once, at Dadeland Mall. Moses Somebody-or-other.
Gimme a break. If I was gonna join a cult, it would
be the Children of Granny Feelgood. "Do it if it feels
good." Yeah, I'll worship her, man.

(**WADE** *quietly takes the Heart album from* **TAMMY** *and
puts it away.*)

TAMMY *(cont.)* Hey, I'm on her side. That's what I'm saying.
Compared to what she was into before, your parents
should be *glad* now.

WADE. They don't want us to even talk about her.

TAMMY. That's so... out of proportion, man.

WADE. Well, they're on drugs, too. I mean, Allison and
Steve. I like to imagine they're living somewhere where
it snows. Somewhere that looks old-fashioned and real,
not like Miami. And that they're trying to go clean. But
now Chip does all the same stuff, and even worse –

TAMMY. And your parents couldn't give a shit, right? That's
such a double standard. My mom said that your dad
almost acted like he thought it was *funny.* It's okay for
his son, the man, to knock up some slut, but it's not
okay for his precious daughter to fuckin shack up with
her boyfriend? That stinks to high heaven, if you ask
me. What is this supposed to be, like, the *fifties*?

WADE. I know.

TAMMY. It's great for you, though.

WADE. Why?

TAMMY. Well, I mean, you're a son, too. You've got a free pass. What are you waiting for? There's plenty of girls who'd love to break you in.

WADE. I'm too skinny.

TAMMY. For what? Look at Mick Jagger. You're a total cutie, Wade. Don't you know that?

WADE. I'm skinny and I don't have any muscles.

TAMMY. There's only one muscle you need, and it actually looks bigger on skinny guys. You're even cuter when you turn all red like that. Come on, Wade. You're like, sixteen already, right? Have you even kissed a girl? You haven't, have you? Oh, shit. Well… would you like to try? I mean, we wouldn't have to tell anyone. It could be just between us. Don't you wanna try? Chip said he started when he was, like, twelve.

(She moves in. He evades her.)

WADE. Speaking of Chip…

TAMMY. I'm so sick of him. I'm gonna break up with him tonight.

WADE. After you break up with him, maybe we can –

TAMMY. Why are you so shy? Just one kiss.

WADE. Why do you wanna do this?

TAMMY. You still don't trust me. I really like you, Wade. You don't treat me like I belong, like, *over there*. You know? Don't you wanna kiss me?

(She leans in to him. He closes his eyes and meets her half way. They share an awkward kiss.

She takes his hand and places it on her breast.)

TAMMY *(cont.)* Feel me up if you want.

(He leaves his hand where she placed it.)

Move your hand around. Like, squeeze and pinch and stuff. Get creative. You've got a boner, don't you?

(He takes his hand away.)

TAMMY (*cont.*) Okay, I'll shut up.

(*He puts his hand back on her breast, then tries to kiss her again, but only brushes the side of her face. He puts the other hand on the other breast, tries to move his hands around, studying his own actions with scientific curiosity.* **TAMMY** *watches him with growing concern.*)

TAMMY (*cont.*) Are you getting into it yet?

WADE. Chip might come back.

TAMMY. He went to Overtown. It'll be, like, awhile. C'mon.

(**WADE** *kisses the side of Tammy's neck, but bumps her head with his.*)

Ow. I see why you hit a lot of cones.

(**WADE** *pulls away.*)

I'm kidding. C'mon, lighten up. That's the only way it works. Here.

(**TAMMY** *pulls Wade's T-shirt over his head before he can stop her, and tosses it behind her. He tries to cover his underdeveloped torso with his spindly arms.*)

I like it. You look good. Try the nipples. That always works.

(**WADE** *pinches his own nipples.*)

TAMMY (*cont.*) Oh. Okay, but I meant –

(*Suddenly, the Cuckoo clock goes off eight times.* **TAMMY** *has a fit of uncontrollable laughter.* **WADE** *tries to grab his T-shirt back.*)

WADE. Leave me alone!

TAMMY. I'm sorry! It was just soooo funny! You had your elbows out, like, when you imitate a chicken, and then that clucking noise started. I couldn't help it!

WADE. Let me have my shirt back. I mean it.

(**TAMMY** *hands him his shirt. He puts it back on, with obvious relief, then turns around shakily and drifts toward the coffee table. A long pause.*)

cut to

TAMMY. *(gently)* You really *don't* like girls, do you?

WADE. *(hotly protesting)* What?!

TAMMY. Hey. It's okay.

WADE. You better take that back!

TAMMY. Wade, it's okay.

WADE. I'm not!

TAMMY. *(to cheer him up)* I say "Fuck Anita Bryant," man! Slap another pie in her face and run her outta town!

WADE. I don't care!

TAMMY. I'm still boycotting orange juice. She can plant that Florida Sunshine Tree where the sun *don't* shine!

WADE. Cut it out.

TAMMY. I mean it. That bitch really pissed me off. Our own home town did something so cool, and she turns around and screws it up in front of the whole country. I bet your parents voted… oh… shit. You poor thing.

WADE. Just leave me alone!

TAMMY. Don't worry. I won't say anything.

WADE. There's nothing to say! I like girls! I just don't like sluts!

*(**TAMMY** glares at him. **WADE** starts clearing the glasses of Seven-Up off the table.)*

WADE. *(cont.)* Maybe you better go wait in the room – on Chip's side.   *P. 38*

(He exits through the dining room with the glasses.
***TAMMY** throws herself onto the sofa.*

She pulls a baggie out of her tight jeans' pocket, and expertly rolls a joint.

***WADE** enters.)*

WADE. What do you think you're doing?

TAMMY. I'm sitting on the couch so it won't be lonely.

(She plops her feet on the coffee table.)

WADE. Get your feet off there.

TAMMY. That's no way to talk to a visiting dignitary. The ambassador from Slutland.

(*She finishes rolling the joint.*)

WADE. You can't do that in here!

TAMMY. You said I could smoke. You didn't say *what*.

WADE. At least go do it in the room.

TAMMY. No, I like where I am.

WADE. You better not light that!

(*She lights the joint.*)

You better not burn any holes in that couch!

TAMMY. No prob.

(*She drags the ashtray toward herself.*)

What is this, an ashtray or a manhole cover?

WADE. (*fanning the air*) You're gonna get Chip in trouble, you know.

TAMMY. That should make you happy.

WADE. Please. Put it out. Look, Tammy. I'm sorry I called you a slut, but it's not like you didn't call *yourself* one, like numerous times.

TAMMY. You sure are learning a lot about people from those books, boy.

WADE. What's that supposed to mean?

TAMMY. My fuckin point exactly. Maybe I was wrong, what I said. Maybe you do like girls, but if you do, you're too goddamn afraid to do anything about it. You're afraid of everything.

WADE. No, I'm not.

TAMMY. Alright, then let me see you take a hit right now.

WADE. I don't like pot.

TAMMY. How do you know, if you never tried?

WADE. I don't like the smell.

(**WADE** *opens the front door and swings it, for ventilation.*)

TAMMY. You will once you've tried it.

cut to—

WADE. Look. Just forget it. I'm not gonna try every stupid thing you ask me to. / *Cut from*

TAMMY. Suit yourself.

WADE. Please put it out. You're gonna cause a big problem here. I said I was sorry. Come on, Tammy, this is really serious.

TAMMY. OKAY!

(She takes one last, long draw, and carefully stubs out the joint in the ashtray.)

Then, do you at least have something alcoholic?

WADE. No!

TAMMY. God.

(WADE exits, and returns with a can of air freshener. He sprays the room generously, explaining himself to her, though she is not by any means forgiven.)

WADE. Look, it's not like I'm *afraid.* I mean, I never smoked pot, but I did inhale once. The smoke. At the Jefferson Starship concert. People all around me were smoking it, and I started to feel kinda funny. I was with my friend Shelly, and sometimes she would say something to me, but I didn't ever respond, because I couldn't be sure if she had just said the thing, or if it was awhile ago, so I thought it might not make sense to answer at the moment, you know, like I could suddenly say, "My bike basket," or whatever, and she might not know what I was talking about.

TAMMY. *(grudgingly; he's not forgiven, either)* That doesn't happen to me, but I've heard of it. Congratulations. You were high.

WADE. Good. Then I know for sure that I don't like it.

TAMMY. I think that's enough spray.

WADE. I hope so.

(He casts Tammy an ornery glance, picks up the ashtray, and carries it toward the dining room.)

TAMMY. There's a roach in that ashtray!

*(Startled, **WADE** drops it on the floor. It breaks into several pieces.)*

TAMMY *(cont.)* Not that kind!

*(**TAMMY** erupts with laughter.)*

Oh, man, you really don't like bugs, do you?

WADE. Damn. It broke.

TAMMY. On all this…plush… whatchamacallit? Must be cheap as shit. Oh, God, look at all those ashes.

WADE. Don't rub. It might stain the carpet. I better go get the vacuum.

TAMMY. Wait 'til I find the roach, okay?

*(**TAMMY** searches the carpet for the butt of her joint.)*

Man, this is like friggin grass. My grass fell in the grass.

*(**TAMMY** tries to get **WADE** to laugh, but he's far too upset.*

He tries desperately to piece the ashtray back together. She watches him awhile. Her laughter fades.)

TAMMY *(cont.)* Sometimes I laugh when I shouldn't. I can't help it.

(beat; he doesn't respond.)

I'll grab the ciggy butts too, so they don't clog the vacuum cleaner. Okay?

(beat; he still doesn't answer.)

Look, Wade, I'm really sorry. For the ashtray, and for… anything I might've, you know, *said*. You can dish it out, for sure, but I'm the one who knows better. So, I'm sorry. Okay?

WADE. *(a long beat; softening)* This reminds me of the time Allison lost her earring in here. We looked for hours, crawling around on all fours.

TAMMY. You really miss her, don't you?

WADE. That's why I don't like Heart anymore. That song, Magic Man. It's like, the very thing that happened to her, with Steve. Telling her to come home with him awhile and get high. And my mom did cry a couple times. Just not on the phone.

TAMMY. It's amazing how music gets so deep, you know? Like you can really feel that it's telling your own exact story. I cry whenever I hear *Rainy Days and Mondays*.

WADE. The Carpenters?

TAMMY. Yeah. What, are you surprised? She has the best voice in the world. Joni Mitchell's great, too. But, you know, if you really listen to her songs…she's no goody two-shoes.

WADE. That's such a dumb expression. How many shoes do bad people wear?

TAMMY. (*chuckling lightly*) You really are funny. I'm just saying. Don't knock Heart. Joni Mitchell sings about sex, drugs, and rock and roll, too.

WADE. Yeah, but at least she doesn't sound *happy* about it.

TAMMY. Allison's okay, Wade. She's *nineteen*.

(*A long beat.*)

WADE. I remember one time, a couple years ago, Chip was really bugging me, and Allison just looks at me and goes, "Get in my car." She got this old Buick Riviera when she turned 16. It was a total boat, all rusty, but it ran. My mom used it once to plow down our Christmas Palms when they got lethal yellowing. Anyway, Allison drove me to Matheson Hammock park and we just sat there under the skunk trees with the Spanish moss and laughed and talked. She always listened to whatever I wanted to say. Then suddenly she had to go to the bathroom really bad, but the bathrooms were locked, so we ran to the car, and started to drive home. I told her she should stop at a gas station but she wouldn't. Every time we got to a red light, she'd stop way short, just so that she could inch forward and stop again a few times until it turned green. Like, she just needed to keep her legs busy. I was trying so hard to keep a straight face, but I couldn't help it. The car just jerked one time too

many and I busted out laughing. Allison got mad and
called me a name, you know, like Chip always does,
except that was the only time she ever said it. We were
both really completely quiet the rest of the way. Then
she pulled into the yard and just put it in park right in
the grass, and ran inside. After she got out of the bathroom, she came to find me, and she was crying, and
she said she was really sorry for calling me *that name*. I
know she meant it – the apology, not the name.

(*beat*)

She was the only one around here who ever apolo-
gized. Until you.

TAMMY. I sure wish I knew her.

(*Another long beat.*)

WADE. Tammy, you don't really think I'm *that way*, do you?

TAMMY. What? Oh, I… guess not. You know what, though?
It doesn't bother me, if somebody is. Especially for,
like, blow jobs. A mouth is a mouth, right? There
aren't male mouths and female mouths.

WADE. But I don't want anyone to think I'm like that. Chip's
always saying it, and so do the jocks in P.E. It's not fair.
I get along much better with girls. How could I not *like*
them?

TAMMY. You care too much about what people think. If I
were you, the next time Chip called me a faggot – him
or any of those assholes in P.E. – I'd haul off and kiss
'em right on the fuckin lips.

(**WADE** *giggles, turns red, and resumes searching.*)

Here we go!

(*She finds the roach, blows the lint off it and puts it in
her pocket.*)

WADE. My mom's going to kill me. She got this ashtray
in Spain. There's this whole story about how my dad
snuck out and bought it for her while she was napping
at the hotel. She tells everybody who comes over.

TAMMY. You can say I broke it. It's kinda true.

WADE. Or we can just go downtown and get a manhole cover.

(*They giggle conspiratorially.*

The front door opens, and **CHIP** *enters. He's a bit hopped up.*)

CHIP. What's happenin, man? Playin fuckin Twister without the mat?

(*He notices the broken ashtray.*)

No way! Mom's Spanish ashtray! Man, are you in for it.

(**TAMMY** *rises, placing the cigarette butts on the coffee table.*)

TAMMY. You took long enough.

CHIP. (*sniffing*) You guys been gettin high?

TAMMY. I was.

CHIP. In here? I told you to wait in my room.

TAMMY. I was talkin to your brother, do you mind?

CHIP. What did you girls talk about?

TAMMY. You son of a –

WADE. (*cutting her off*) Nothing –

(**WADE** *silently beseeches* **TAMMY** *not to start trouble.*)

CHIP. You two got some kinda secret language goin on?

TAMMY. Massachusetts. How's that for a secret language?

CHIP. What the fuck you been talkin about?

(**WADE** *carries the broken pieces of the ashtray to a decorative wastebasket beside the couch.*)

WADE. I wanted to know about snow.

TAMMY. The kind that falls from the sky, you bastard.

WADE. Tam –

TAMMY. Your brother told me what you tried to do. What you said to get fuckin *money*.

CHIP. (*to Wade*) You motherfucker, you promised –

TAMMY. You think you can just talk about it however you want? Like it's *your* thing to talk about however the hell you want?

CHIP. Who said –

(*to* **WADE**)

I'm gonna kick your ass!

WADE. I didn't –

TAMMY. He was just tryin to help. He didn't know the truth.

CHIP. Tryin to help nothin!

TAMMY. 'Cuz there was nothin to help! 'Cuz you friggin *lied*.

CHIP. It was partly true.

TAMMY. That clump of cells landed in that bottle. That's what's true.

CHIP. (*to* **WADE**) You're in deep shit, Sherlock.

TAMMY. Stop tryin to put it off on him. You're the one who did this. How could you say it? How could you, like, form any words out loud about it still being alive?

(*to* **WADE**)

What was the look on his face? How did he look when he talked about it?

WADE. I better stay out of this.

CHIP. Too late for that, big mouth.

(*to* **TAMMY**)

Look, I wanted to get some money for us. So we could have a good time. Get our minds off Massachusetts.

TAMMY. Easy for you.

CHIP. When did you ever say you didn't wanna go to Massachusetts?

TAMMY. That's because –

CHIP. No, when? Tell me, when did you *once* hesitate? You might not like what I think about you, but I only think what I think 'cuz of what I see.

TAMMY. Then see this.

(*She heads for the door.*)

CHIP. What am I supposed to be lookin' at?

TAMMY. Me walkin out of your miserable stupid-ass life.

CHIP. Walkin is right. I ain't drivin you anywhere.

TAMMY. Your brother is twice the man you are, even if –

(Tammy exits.)

CHIP. Thanks alot, dufus.

WADE. How's she gonna get home?

CHIP. That's her problem now.

WADE. You better go get her.

CHIP. She'll be back.

WADE. I don't think so. She seemed pretty pissed.

*(**CHIP** pulls a baggie of white powder out of his jeans pocket.)*

CHIP. If she wants any of this, she'll be back.

WADE. Is that cocaine?

CHIP. Or something. Never you mind. And if you tell anybody I showed you, I'll kick your ass.

WADE. Why did you *show* me?

CHIP. I don't know.

WADE. What is it?

CHIP. Like I'm gonna tell you, blabbermouth?

WADE. Look, I don't think she's coming back. If you're not gonna go –

*(There's a knock at the door, then it opens. **TAMMY** enters, with tears in her eyes.)*

CHIP. Told ya.

*(He approaches her smugly. She ignores him, and approaches **WADE**.)*

TAMMY. I need to use your phone.

CHIP. Tell 'er the phone costs a dime.

TAMMY. Tell him that's ten times what he's worth.

WADE. You're both upset. You should calm down so you can talk about it.

CHIP. Peace talks are for pussies.

WADE. Stop repeating what dad says!

(**TAMMY** *picks up the phone.* **WADE** *stops her with a gesture.*)

Tammy, wait. I bet you both are feeling a lot more the same than you think right now. What you went through… it's practically an *ordeal*!

(**CHIP**'s *indignant posture slackens.* **TAMMY** *puts the receiver down.*)

TAMMY. Well, we basically created, like, *life* together. If there's anything you wanna say to me…

(**CHIP** *hesitates. She picks up the phone again.*)

CHIP. (*soberly*) Alright. Come back to my room.

TAMMY. No. Here.

CHIP. Alright, then, Wade, go to our room.

TAMMY. No. He stays.

CHIP. I ain't sayin anything in front of him.

TAMMY. This all started 'cuz of something you said to him. You need to get it straight with both of us.

(**TAMMY** *stands next to* **WADE**. *They present a united front.*)

CHIP. I ain't talkin in front of him. Now, you wanna hear me or not?

TAMMY. Do you even have anything to say worth hearing?

CHIP. (*with winning sincerity*) Yeah, I do.

(**CHIP** *hangs his head and seems almost on the verge of tears. Surprised and softened,* **TAMMY** *hangs up the phone and drifts away from* **WADE**. *She takes* **CHIP** *by the arm.*

Behind Tammy's back, **CHIP** *sticks his tongue out at* **WADE** *with an amused sneer, and the pair disappear down the hall.*

WADE *lingers in the foyer listening as their hushed voices emanate from the hallway.*

Whispers are soon followed by sounds of youthful passion.

WADE *dials the phone.)*

WADE. Lynnette Minnick, please. It's her son. ... Hi, Mom. Chip brought Tammy here again. ... Yes, she's back. But Chip's been lying, and I have proof, and there's a lot going on that you should know about, and they didn't go to the movies, and now they're in our room making out. ... It's my room, too. It's revolting. ... He's – I'm sure he's doing something else, too, just like I said. ... How are you supposed to know if I don't tell you? ... So you can do something about it! ... I guess I just wasn't born to be attractive!

*(***WADE** *hangs up and exits through the dining room.*

He returns a moment later with a vacuum, plugs it in and and turns it on. The machine barely drowns out the moans and groans coming from the hallway.)

(Lights fade.)

End of Act One

ACT TWO

Scene One

(A while later. In the dark, the cuckoo calls nine times. Then, a voice is heard speaking mechanically in French. "Ou vont vos voisins en vacances?" Lights fade up on **WADE** *as he repeats the phrase with an unconvincing accent. A bucket, a rag and a spray bottle sit on the floor near where the ashes were spilled.)*

WADE. *Ou vont vos voisins en vacances?* Where are your neighbors going on vacation?

TAPE. Where will your neighbors go on holiday? *Ils vont en Italie.*

WADE. *Ils vont en Italie.* They are going to Italy.

TAPE. They are going to Italy. *Ils vont en Espagne.*

WADE. *Ils vont en Espagne.* Spain. They're going to Spain.

*(***CHIP*** enters, shirtless and in jeans from the hallway carrying dumbbells.)*

TAPE. They are going to Spain. *Ils vont aux Etats-Unis.*

*(***CHIP*** lies on the floor and starts to do chest presses.)*

WADE. You're not supposed to do that out here.

CHIP. Tammy's crashin.

TAPE. They are going to the United States. *Ils vont en Allemagne.*

WADE. I'm trying to study.

CHIP. *(mimicking French sounds) Fahn fahn fahn fahn.*

TAPE. They are going to Germany. *Allemagne de l'Est, ou Allemagne de l'Ouest?*

CHIP. Dad call yet?

WADE. No.

TAPE. East Germany, or West Germany? *Allemagne de l'Ouest, bien sur!*

CHIP. He musta called and you didn't hear it. It's already nine.

TAPE. West Germany, of course!

CHIP. Of course!

WADE. The tape's not that loud. Believe me. The phone didn't ring.

CHIP. Mr. Punctuality must be slippin.

TAPE. *Comment vont-ils?*

(**WADE** *turns off the tape.*)

WADE. I guess Tammy's not mad at you anymore. What did you say to her?

CHIP. None of your beeswax, Smedley.

WADE. Take those weights out of here.

CHIP. You should do a few reps. You could use it.

WADE. I'd rather build up my mind.

CHIP. That's *so...* You probably couldn't even lift these.

WADE. What's she sleeping for? She probably got bored because you don't have a mind.

CHIP. No, she smoked a roach and zonked out. Anyway, it ain't my mind she likes.

WADE. She would if you had one.

CHIP. What do you know about girls?

WADE. Tammy talked to me a lot when you were gone.

CHIP. So I gathered.

WADE. You can't be pissed at me. From what *you* told *me.* I was trying to help.

CHIP. I know, I know.

WADE. I just can't believe you told me that. After what *really* happened.

CHIP. I fucked up, okay? Just shut up about it.

WADE. Tammy needs –

CHIP. Don't you tell me what Tammy needs. Just 'cuz you guys had one conversation doesn't mean you suddenly have any say in anything. Just butt out.

WADE. But I wanna ask you something. She told me about dad.

CHIP. Yeah?

WADE. So… he actually paid for it?

CHIP. Yeah.

WADE. Does mom know?

CHIP. I'm pretty sure she doesn't. Look, I don't wanna talk about this. It's none of your business. You wouldn't understand anyway.

WADE. I'm only a year younger than you.

CHIP. Yeah, but there's a lot you don't know. Hopefully you'll never know.

WADE. But I have a right. He's my dad, too.

CHIP. Go back to your *fahn fahn fahn.*

WADE. Shut up.

(**WADE** *turns the tape back on.*)

TAPE. How are they going? *Ils prennent le train.*

WADE. *(having a hard time with the 'r's)* Ils prennent le train.

CHIP. You sound like shit.

WADE. Like to hear you try it.

CHIP. *(a perfect imitation of the French)* Ils prennent le train.

(**WADE**'s *smug expression fades.*)

TAPE. They are taking the train.

CHIP. Sure they are.

TAPE. *Ils prennent l'autobus.*

WADE. I just don't see how he can be like this about Allison all this time, if he's not even mad at you.

(*The phone rings.*)

CHIP. There he is. I dare you to say that to him.

(**WADE** *heads for it, but stops short.*)

TAPE. They are taking the bus. *Ils vont par avion.*

CHIP. Chicken.

WADE. I'm turning the tape off.

*(**WADE** does so. **CHIP** answers the phone.)*

CHIP. Fahn fahn fahn fahn? … Hey, dad. What's up? … Nothin. Just listenin to Wade butcher the French language. …. No. … Bridge. Right, Wade? … Yeah, she's at bridge. … You gonna be in town for my match on Sunday? I'm playin Tim Stokes. He's number three seed. I'm gonna clean his clock. Thought you might like to watch. … I know. … I know, I've been workin on it. … Dad, my backhand – … Alright, then, play him yourself. Think you could pass for 18 and under with that gut? … No, it rained today. Grass was too wet. I'll do it tomorrow. … Don't worry, dad, it'll be done before you get back. … Yeah, I've seen her. Tonight. We went to the movies. … Seargent Pepper's. … I won't, I swear. … Yep, I got, like, a year's supply. Dad, I know what I'm doin. You wanna fill in for me there, too? … What? What do you mean?

(Chip's arrogant chuckle abruptly stops. He looks stunned and wounded by something his father has said, and at a loss for a response. A look of rage grows on his face.

*Concerned, **WADE** reaches for the phone. **CHIP** slams the receiver against the edge of the table. **WADE** grabs it.)*

WADE. Hi, dad, it's Wade. … Nothing. Chip just dropped the phone. … She's at bridge. … Call her there, if you want. Do you need the number? … *She's there*, dad. … Hey, wanna hear something funny? Today in French class, this girl Nina, she was saying "luh," because "the" is either "le" or "la" depending on masculine and feminine. And she wasn't sure which one it was, so she kept saying "luh," kinda to split the difference. She totally got away with it. The teacher just corrected her pronunciation, without realizing Nina didn't know which one it really was. So one time, when it was my turn, I said – … Oh, sorry. But I was almost done. … Never mind. Now that I think of it, it wasn't that funny. Okay, well – … I know. I'll rake it as soon as he mows. Like always. It kinda has to go in that order, right? … Okay. I love you. … thanks.

(**WADE** *hangs up. Both brothers stare at the phone.*)

WADE *(cont.)* You better mow the yard tomorrow or we'll *both* get it.

CHIP. Yeah, right. Fuck him!

WADE. You're lucky you didn't break the phone. What did dad say to you?

CHIP. He's an asshole.

WADE. What are you so mad about?

CHIP. I don't wanna talk about it. I'm gettin outta here. Outta fuckin Dodge.

WADE. Like *you* have it so bad.

CHIP. You don't know shit.

WADE. Then tell me.

CHIP. *(to himself)* Motherfucker.

(**CHIP** *takes out the baggie, pours out some of the powder, cuts two lines on the coffee table and snorts them with a small straw.*)

WADE. What are you doing? Stop that!

CHIP. Get off my back, you little wussy.

WADE. Why? You always call me names, and give me a hard time, and it makes no sense. Chip, I'm your only brother. Your little brother. You should be wanting to teach me things. Why won't you talk to me about anything that *matters*?

CHIP. Because you *are* my little brother. Because I gotta protect you.

WADE. How are you gonna protect anybody when you're all doped up?

CHIP. You don't know shit.

WADE. Then *tell me* shit.

CHIP. Just leave me the fuck alone.

WADE. Are you jones-ing?

CHIP. There's that damn g again. It's jones-in. Nobody ever says they're jones-*ing*. Look. I'm not in a very good mood, but you don't jones until you run outta dope. There. I taught you somethin. Now get off my case.

WADE. At least help me clean your girlfriend's cigarette ashes out of the carpet.

CHIP. You're the domestic one, sweetie. Don't tell me you've been waitin all this time for me to help.

WADE. No, I was letting it soak, but –

CHIP. Great. You seem to know what you're doin. Go for it.

(**CHIP** *resumes weight-lifting.*)

WADE. Are dad and mom having a fight?

CHIP. What?

WADE. He kept asking where she was, like he didn't believe us, when we both told him at least twice.

CHIP. What?

WADE. Why do you keep saying what?

CHIP. What?

WADE. Stop it. Do you know what I'm saying?

CHIP. Fuckin horndog.

WADE. What?

CHIP. Bang fuckin Pollyanna.

WADE. What?

CHIP. Dad. You think he ain't out ballin stewardesses? "I'm Nancy, fly me."

WADE. He is not!

CHIP. You're such a baby. He's out fuckin around, that's why he thinks she is. I'm sick of all this shit.

WADE. This is not coming out.

CHIP. Just need some elbow grease, man.

(**CHIP** *drops the weights, grabs a rag and scrubs the rug roughly.*)

WADE. Use a circular motion, and not so hard.

CHIP. Is that what you do?

(**CHIP** *mimics jerking off, moaning in a high pitch.*

He pursues this line of torment out of habit, with none of the usual enjoyment.)

WADE. Stop it! I don't do that!

CHIP. The fuck you don't! I do it too, man. Everybody does.

WADE. I don't. It's disgusting.

CHIP. Are you kiddin me? Look, I know you do. I'm not always asleep when you think I am.

WADE. It's like what you said about dad and mom. You just think I do that because you do.

CHIP. Wade, every guy jerks off, unless they're a total idiot. There's nothin to be ashamed of. Didn't dad talk to you about that?

WADE. Why? Did he talk to you?

CHIP. Yeah. Long time ago. Man.

WADE. What?

CHIP. All this time, you've been thinkin it's not okay or somethin?

WADE. I can't figure out what's okay and what's not anymore.

CHIP. Dad shoulda told you.

WADE. He never talks to me.

CHIP. I think he just doesn't *get* you. You know?

WADE. What's to get? I do everything I'm supposed to do.

CHIP. Yeah. Nobody knows what to make of that.

WADE. How does anybody win? You do something they don't like, and you're no longer their child. But you do everything they want, and you're, like, a martian. Except for you. You do whatever the hell you want and they still fall all over you.

CHIP. You don't know. You don't have somebody on you all the time. Be the best. Win! Win! And even if you win, it's like, that was too close. You shoulda beat 'em by a mile. Ruth Buzzi has a better backhand. And then, it's like, what kind of cheap hag is this you're goin out with? Her face is like sandpaper. No granchild of mine is poppin out of that dog. But still you can see the drool at the corner of his mouth. He's a sick bastard. I hate his fuckin guts and I don't ever wanna see him again.

WADE. Then why'd you invite him to your match this weekend?

CHIP. Well… that's just to throw him off. I'll be long gone by then. I'm gettin outta Dodge.

WADE. Running away?

CHIP. Whatever, man. Leavin.

WADE. Tammy's going with you?

CHIP. That's what I should do. Knock her up again and marry her ass. Like to see his face then.

WADE. Chip, did you… not really want that abortion?

CHIP. Are you nuts? Me, have a kid?

WADE. Maybe that's why you told me Tammy was still pregnant. You wanted it to be true.

CHIP. Alright, Dr. Joyce fuckin Brothers.

(**CHIP** *scrubs harder at the carpet.*)

WADE. Don't! You're grinding it in.

CHIP. Ancient Chinese secret!

WADE. It's not funny! Mom's gonna kill us!

(**CHIP** *throws the rag down, grabs* **WADE** *by the arm and pulls him to where the weights lay.*)

CHIP. Pick 'em up.

WADE. What?

CHIP. Pick 'em up. I want to see you do at least ten.

WADE. I don't want –

CHIP. Do it!

(**WADE** *struggles to lift the weights over his head.* **CHIP**

gets behind him and helps guide his arms. **WADE**
manages to get them up once, but lets his arms drop
afterward.)

CHIP *(cont.)* You gotta let 'em down easy. C'mon, nine
more.

WADE. Chip, I can't.

CHIP. Do it!

*(**WADE** tries again. This time, **CHIP** has to help him*
*more. **WADE** manages to let them down slower.)*

CHIP *(cont.)* That was better. Eight more.

WADE. I can't.

*(**WADE** gives up half way through the lift. **CHIP** com-*
pletes it for him.)

CHIP. Seven more.

*(**CHIP** lifts and lowers the weights rapidly, his hands*
over Wade's.)

WADE. Let me get out of your way.

CHIP. Six more!

WADE. Chip, forget it.

CHIP. Five more!

WADE. *(losing patience)* You're doing it all yourself! Let go,
you're hurting my fingers.

*(**CHIP** lets go while the weights are high in the air. They*
*crash to the floor, pulling **WADE** down with them.)*

CHIP. You just better get ready. I'm leavin, so you gotta take
care of yourself from now own.

WADE. You can't leave! You're gonna graduate in six
months!

CHIP. You're the schoolmarm, not me. I mean it. I'm packin
up and gettin the hell outta Dodge.

WADE. No, you can't.

CHIP. Watch me.

WADE. I'm gonna call mom at bridge.

CHIP. Don't you have homework to do?

(**CHIP** *exits down the hall.*)

WADE. What are you gonna do? Chip?

> (*There's no answer.* **WADE** *hovers near the phone.*

> **CHIP** *enters again with a pillowcase crammed full of clothes. He heads for the front door.*)

WADE *(cont.)* What's that? Where are you going?

> (**CHIP** *exits.* **WADE** *follows him out the front door. A car door is heard opening and closing.*

> **CHIP** *enters followed by* **WADE.**)

WADE *(cont.)* You can't do this to mom!

CHIP. Like she gives a fat rat's ass.

WADE. Thanksgiving is in two weeks!

> (**CHIP** *lets out a bitter guffaw and disappears down the hall.*

> **WADE** *picks up the phone, but hesitates.* **CHIP** *returns with another bundle wrapped in a blanket.* **WADE** *hangs up.*)

CHIP. I know you weren't callin mom.

WADE. Just stay 'til Thanksgiving. And then Christmas. Don't ruin the holidays, Chip, please!

CHIP. I ain't celebratin the birth of Christ with a dude who thinks he *is* Christ.

WADE. You can't run away. First Allison and now you.

CHIP. They don't give a shit. They're prob'ly countin the days 'til you and me are gone. Dad's all strict with us three days a week, then, the other four, he's off bangin' stewardesses around the world like there's no tomorrow. Once we're gone, he can get his turtle waxed six days a week, and on the seventh, he shall rest.

WADE. He's not like that! Mom wouldn't stay with somebody like that!

CHIP. Oh, you wanna talk about mom? She couldn't care less what happens around here. All she does is play fuckin bridge.

WADE. I know, but she does care!

CHIP. Bullshit! She plays bridge 'cuz she wants to be a life fuckin master so she has somethin to talk about when she meets Omar Sharif and runs off with him on his yacht.

WADE. She cried and cried about Allison!

CHIP. Prob'ly jealous. Wishes *she* could hit the road. In fact, she prob'ly will pretty soon anyway. All those losers at the bridge club slobberin all over her.

WADE. You're crazy. You're just… on drugs. It makes you see everything all distorted and wrong. Everything around here is normal.

CHIP. Who said it wasn't?

WADE. You're not making sense.

CHIP. See, you ask me to tell you things, to be your teacher, and then you don't wanna learn. You're a hopeless case.

WADE. I know you're making this up. Dad musta really made you mad on the phone. What did he say? If you won't tell me anything else, just at least tell me that.

CHIP. That's what I ain't ever gonna tell you.

WADE. I'll call mom at bridge.

CHIP. Why don't you just go beat it to your Tiger Beat. "Oh, Shawn Cassidy, I love you!"

WADE. I don't love Shawn Cassidy!

CHIP. You tell anybody I'm leavin, I'll tell 'em you beat off to Shawn Cassidy's picture.

WADE. Liar!

CHIP. Faggot.

WADE. What did you say?

(**TAMMY** *appears groggily from the hallway.*)

CHIP. I said, you're a faggot.

TAMMY. Hey, c'mon, you guys. What's goin on around here?

WADE. He just called me a faggot, Tammy.

CHIP. Damn right.

WADE. I just wanted to make sure that's what you said.

CHIP. What?

> (**WADE** *smiles meaningfully at Tammy.* **CHIP** *looks to Tammy, questioning.* **TAMMY** *shrugs.*
>
> **WADE** *grabs Chip's face and plants a big kiss on his lips. Chip's body jerks for a second, then he relaxes and closes his eyes.*
>
> *Unresisted,* **WADE** *hold the kiss a little longer than necessary. He pulls away, shaking.*)

CHIP *(cont.)* Not bad. Now lick my nips.

> (**CHIP** *guides Wade's head toward his gorgeous chest.* **WADE** *frees himself.*)

WADE. Put a shirt on, you Neanderthal!

CHIP. I like "the situation is reversed" better.

WADE. I thought you were getting out of Dodge. Why don't you?

CHIP. I better. Before I get fuckin raped.

WADE. That's all you know. I only did that 'cuz Tammy told me to. Right after she let me feel her up!

TAMMY. Wade!

> *(to* **CHIP***)*

> I felt sorry for him.

CHIP. Uh-huh.

> (**CHIP** *drops the bundle and glares at them both. A long beat.*)

CHIP *(cont.) (to* **WADE***)* Well? How was it?

WADE. I… um…

CHIP. Did it float your boat? She's got nice tits, huh?

TAMMY. You bastard.

CHIP. So who'd you like better, Wade? Her, or me?

TAMMY. Don't you care about *anything*?

CHIP. What do you want me to do? Get pissed off at you? Haul off and slug your ass?

WADE. You better not hit anybody, or I'll –

CHIP. You'll what? Wussy.

(CHIP grabs WADE by the collar of his T-shirt.)

TAMMY. Leave him alone!

CHIP. Oh, I'm the bad guy, huh? Here he is, tellin me I don't know how to be a brother, and in the meantime he's feelin up my girlfriend. If that's bein a brother, then, yeah, I guess I don't know how. I'd never do that shit to you, man.

(WADE doesn't know what to say.)

You can have 'er, because I'm leavin.

(He picks up the bundle and heads out the front door again. WADE approaches TAMMY consolingly.)

TAMMY. Get away from me!

(CHIP enters empty-handed. Heads for the hallway.)

Chip –

CHIP. Stay clear if you know what's good for you.

(CHIP exits down the hall.)

WADE. I'm sorry.

TAMMY. Try to be nice, and look what I get.

WADE. He made me mad, and it just came out.

TAMMY. That's supposed to make it all better?

WADE. Well, it wasn't against you.

TAMMY. No. It had nothing to do with me. That's worse.

WADE. I'll go talk to him.

TAMMY. I think you've done enough talking.

(CHIP enters with his stereo. He is flying high now. Wiping his nose, he almost drops the stereo. TAMMY helps him catch it.)

TAMMY *(cont.)* Shit. You did some more of that blow, didn't you?

CHIP. For the road, baby.

WADE. Drugs aren't the answer!

CHIP. Do you hear me askin a question? You sound like a fuckin poster. There's none left for you, Tammy. I woulda shared, but there's been enough sharin around here for one night.

TAMMY. You did it all? Shit.

CHIP. *Now* I'll be jones-in.

WADE. Chip, you can't leave here in this condition.

CHIP. I'm fine, sweetiekins.

WADE. Maybe right now, but…

> (**CHIP** *goes out the front door with the stereo.*)

He's gonna have an accident if he leaves. He could kill somebody.

TAMMY. He won't leave. I got it.

> (**CHIP** *enters again.* **TAMMY** *leans on him suggestively.*)

Hey, Chip, c'mon back to the room. I like you this way. C'mon.

CHIP. Get lost.

TAMMY. No, wait. I didn't mean to wimp out on you before. Let's finish what we started, babe. You're so hot when you're all high. C'mon, it'll be fierce.

CHIP. I thought you said it's too soon.

TAMMY. For *that*, yeah, but…

> (*She presses up against him and whispers into his ear. He grabs her around the waist. She jumps up, wrapping her arms around his neck and her legs around his waist.*
>
> **CHIP** *exits down the hallway, carrying her. Their lustful groans are heard almost immediately.*
>
> **WADE** *goes back to the radio, turns it on, but this time plugs in a pair of headphones with a long cord, and listens through them, so that the room is silent.*
>
> **WADE** *tries to concentrate on his book, but can't.*
>
> *Still wearing the headphones, he inspects the spots on the carpet then takes a carpet rake from a corner and rakes the area carefully.*

Tammy's voice is heard making quick sounds which slowly rise in pitch and volume until words become intelligible.)

TAMMY (O.S.) Stop! Don't! No! Chip, stop! Wade! Wade!

(WADE doesn't hear.

Banging and rifling sounds are heard offstage. The sounds continue throughout the scene. TAMMY runs in, wearing only panties.)

TAMMY *(cont.)* Wade! He's freakin out! Wade!

(She rushes to him, removing the headphones. He looks anywhere but at her breasts.)

Wade, he totally freaked! He couldn't stay hard, and he just went nuts. He ripped that baggie open and licked the inside of it. Now he's, like, tearin your stuff apart.

WADE. What?

(WADE pulls off his T-shirt and hands it to her. She puts it on.)

TAMMY. He's lookin for money. I tried to stop him and he knocked me across the room. Something's really wrong. I don't know what that shit is. Coke or heroin or something. What should we do? I can't go back in there.

WADE. Okay, let's see. Um… do you have his car keys?

TAMMY. No. They're in his jeans, I think.

WADE. Is he… wearing them?

TAMMY. Yeah, he never totally took 'em off.

WADE. I better call my mom.

TAMMY. Wade, this is no time to call your *mommy*!

(WADE quickly explains as he dials.)

WADE. You don't know. He got like this once when you were in Massachusetts. My mom was the only one who could talk him down.

TAMMY. What?

WADE. *(into the phone)* Hi, I need to talk to Lynnette Minnick. It's an emergency. … Her son Wade.

(to **TAMMY**, *in a rapid whisper)*

He told you how he messed up his Firebird, right? He came home all high and rammed the side of the Wilhites' house. Mr. Wilhite was chewing him out in the kitchen. Chip cold-cocked the guy and knocked me down, but my mom stood in front of the door. He couldn't hit her, so he calmed down. She'll talk him down.

TAMMY. Meanwhile, he's totally trashing your side of the room!

WADE. Maybe it'll tire him out.

(into the phone)

Hi, Mom. ... I know, I'm sorry, but you gotta get home. Chip is freaking out again. Worse than the other time. ... No, I was just mad before, but now – I'm not exaggerating. I told you he's on drugs. ... He's throwing stuff around in our room! He might try to drive away. He has the keys to the car. ... I'm not – it's totally *in* proportion! but –

(He hangs up, stunned.)

TAMMY. Is she coming? What did she say?

WADE. *(blandly; in shock)* She's in the middle of a hand.

TAMMY. Wade, I gotta get out of here.

WADE. *(recovering; gesturing to the dining room)* Go through there, you can grab some of my mom's clothes in the master bedroom and then go out the sliding door through the patio. Go right across the street to the Dimarcos and call somebody to come get you.

TAMMY. What are you gonna do?

WADE. I better stay and keep an eye out. If I can get his keys, I'll get out of here. I just don't want him to be able to drive.

TAMMY. I could lock all the car doors when I'm outside.

WADE. He'd just break the window. But, yeah, do that. Try to close the doors so he can't hear it, just in case.

TAMMY. Okay.

(She starts out.)

WADE. And Tammy.

(She pauses at the dining room archway.)

TAMMY. Yeah?

WADE. Don't tell the Dimarcos what's happening. Just say Chip's sick and I don't have my license yet. Oh, and our phone's out of order.

(She looks at him incredulously.)

If they talk to the Wilhites – my parents wouldn't want –

TAMMY. Fuck that noise, man! Fuck your fuckin parents!

*(Suddenly the noises down the hall cease. **TAMMY** and **WADE** exchange one last look, and **TAMMY** flees.*

***WADE** stares toward the hallway holding the carpet rake out defensively. **CHIP** enters in just jeans, looking dazed and exhausted. The bare-chested brothers square off.)*

WADE. Tammy's gone and mom's on her way home.

CHIP. Where's your fuckin money?

WADE. Did you hear me?

CHIP. I need some money.

WADE. I told you I don't have any here.

CHIP. Did mom leave you any?

WADE. No.

CHIP. There's gotta be some somewhere.

*(He starts toward the dining room. **WADE** stands in his way.)*

WADE. Don't go in there.

CHIP. Get out of my way.

WADE. Chip, think about what you're doing.

CHIP. I gotta get some money.

WADE. This is only one night. What are you gonna do every other night?

CHIP. I don't give a shit about any other nights.

WADE. But… they're gonna come anyway. Thousands of them.

CHIP. Get out of my way.

(The sounds of car doors closing one at a time are heard offstage. **WADE** *notices, but is relieved to see that* **CHIP** *doesn't.* **WADE** *steps out of Chip's path.)*

CHIP *(cont.)* If I don't find anything I'm gonna kick your ass.

*(***CHIP** *exits through the dining room. Soon sounds of ransacking are heard again.* **WADE** *looks out the window, then picks up the phone and dials.)*

WADE. Operator, can you connect me with the Dade County police? … Thanks.

(pause; he's on hold)

Hi, I… uh… never mind. Sorry.

(He hangs up and dials another number.)

Lynnette Minnick, please. It's her son again. …. He's starting on *your* room now. Still in the middle of that hand?

(Something breaks offstage. **WADE** *covers his free ear.*

CHIP *reappears in the dining room archway, fuming. His right forearm drips blood.)*

CHIP. Zip!

*(***WADE** *hangs up the phone.)*

WADE. You're bleeding.

CHIP. Not as much as you're gonna be.

(The phone rings. Startled, **CHIP** *picks it up, hangs up and then leaves it off the hook.*

WADE *holds out the rake to protect himself.* **CHIP** *grabs it and tosses it away.)*

WADE. Okay, Chip. I'm gonna give you some money. I don't have a lot, but you can have it all. I'll go get it.

CHIP. *(appeased for the moment)* 'Kay.

WADE. Just come stand in the foyer so your arm can drip on tile.

CHIP. Shit! I'm fuckin bleedin, man!

WADE. Don't worry, I'll help you. Just a minute. Um...

> **(WADE** *exits down the hall.* **CHIP** *stands in the foyer, staring at his reflection. He drums his good hand on the little table, waving the hurt one rapidly in the air.*
>
> *The cuckoo clucks one time, to indicate the half-hour.*
>
> **WADE** *returns with gauze, adhesive tape, a bottle of alcohol and a tissue.)*

WADE. Stop moving your arm around. You're gonna make it worse.

CHIP. Where's the money?

> **(CHIP** *holds out his bloody hand.)*

WADE. Here. You better let me put it in your pocket. If you get blood on money, it's no good anymore.

CHIP. I never heard that.

WADE. If you had a job, you'd know. This is all the money I have.

> **(WADE** *shows* **CHIP** *some bills.* **CHIP** *holds his arm out of the way.* **WADE** *looks at Chip's pockets carefully.)*

WADE *(cont.)* Okay, um... first I'm gonna put some alcohol on your arm so it doesn't get infected.

> **(CHIP** *obeys, holding out his arm.* **WADE** *pours the alcohol liberally over it.)*

CHIP. Ow! Fuck me runnin!

WADE. That means it's working. Now here's the money.

> *(While* **CHIP** *is distracted with pain,* **WADE** *digs into his pocket with one hand, pulling out the car keys, and with the other hand inserting the money. He slips the keys in the pocket of his shorts.)*

CHIP. Aah! Shit! This stings like a motherfucker!

WADE. Sorry, but…

> (**WADE** *daubs the area with a tissue, then dresses the wound.*)

CHIP. Watch where you put that tape! My arm's hairy.

WADE. This is the kind that doesn't hurt when you pull it off.

CHIP. Oh. Thank you, nurse.

WADE. Do you know what you cut it on?

> (**CHIP** *shakes his head, "no."*)

I think you'll need a tetanus shot or something. When mom gets back we better go to the hospital.

CHIP. I ain't gonna be here. You done?

WADE. Yeah.

CHIP. Thanks. Later.

> (**CHIP** *exits out the front door.* **WADE** *takes the keys out of his pocket, and frantically looks for a place to hide them.*)

CHIP (O.S.) *(cont.)* Goddamn it! Wade!

> (**WADE** *hurls the keys behind the entertainment center.* **CHIP** *enters, in a rage.*)

CHIP *(cont.)* Where are my fuckin keys?

WADE. I don't know!

CHIP. What did you do with 'em?

WADE. Nothing! Are they in our room?

CHIP. Where's Tammy?

WADE. She called somebody to come get her, and she walked out. I told you.

CHIP. How long ago was that?

WADE. I don't know. A while ago.

CHIP. Don't play fuckin' games with me, man.

WADE. I'm not!

CHIP. I want my keys!

WADE. I don't have 'em! Maybe you locked 'em inside the car!

CHIP. Shit!

(**CHIP** *starts out, but stops.*)

Wait a second. How did you know all the doors were locked?

WADE. I didn't! I was just guessing.

CHIP. You're fuckin playin games with me, man!

WADE. No!

CHIP. Where'd you put my fuckin KEYS?

(**CHIP** *goes on a frenzied hunt for his keys, ransacking the living room in the process.*)

Where did you put my keys?! I want my keys!

(*When* **CHIP** *heads toward the stereo,* **WADE** *blocks his path.* **CHIP** *knows he's getting warmer.*

CHIP *tears into the stereo cabinets. Wade pounds Chip's back.* **CHIP** *turns and gets* **WADE** *in a half Nelson.* **WADE** *struggles then punches* **CHIP** *in the groin.*)

CHIP *(cont.)* You little shit!

(*Furious,* **CHIP** *takes* **WADE** *to the floor and chokes him.*)

WADE. *(forcing the words out)* I can't breathe!

(*In a blind rage,* **CHIP** *ignores him.* **WADE** *reaches desperately around. His hand finds one of the dumbbells. He tries twice, but can't lift it. The third time, with a loud grunt, he lifts it off the ground, but it falls harmlessly back to the floor. He starts slapping Chip's back with his open hands.*)

WADE *(cont.)* *(in a grotesque whisper)* Okay! Okay! Chip! Uncle! Uncle!

(**CHIP** *comes to himself and releases* **WADE,** *who coughs and gags.* **WADE** *crawls away from him.*)

CHIP. See what you made me do?

(**CHIP** *looks around the spoiled room.*)

Dad's got some major low-hangin balls, tellin *me* I should never be a father. Not just right now. Not just with Tammy. *Never.* Look what a shitty job *he's* doin! Look at us. Look at us right now. And who knows where the hell Allison is, or what shape *she's* in. This is a fuckin disaster. And *he's* gonna tell *me...* I coulda had that kid. I coulda taken care of 'im, and taught 'im things, and he woulda thought I could do no wrong. And when he got older, I woulda let 'im go out for sports and fuckin lose every single time if he sucked, just so long as he kept tryin. And if he didn't wanna go for sports, I'da made sure he did real good in school, so he could do whatever he wanted to do with his life. Even if he was fat, or ugly. I wouldn'a cared. And when he grew up, I'da *wanted* him to have kids, so a part of him would keep goin on. He'da been somethin special. He'da made somethin outta himself. He'd a made somethin outta me.

(CHIP collapses in heaving sobs.)

WADE. I wish I was your kid instead of your brother. Sounds pretty cushy.

CHIP. Sorry for chokin you.

(WADE slowly rises to his feet, goes to the entertainment center, and with a Herculean effort moves it out from the wall enough to reach his arm in. He gets the keys and approaches CHIP carefully.)

WADE. Here are your keys. I'll go with you. Let's go find Allison, and just all take care of each other. Like, we're all each other's kids. I can drive until you... come down, or whatever.

CHIP. You can't drive.

WADE. I have my restricted license. As long as there's a licensed driver in the car with me, I can drive.

CHIP. Okay, well... I'm not feelin too good right now. I think I'm gonna lay down. We'll go later.

(CHIP stumbles out down the hallway.

WADE hangs up the phone and starts spraying the carpet cleaner on Chip's blood drops.

The front door opens. **LYNNETTE** *enters, ready for anything. She realizes that the storm, whatever it might have been, has passed.*

She puts down her purse and approaches **WADE** *apologetically.*

Seeing the marks on his throat, she gasps and reaches out to him. He turns from her and starts to straighten up the place.

She watches her boy a while in silence, then exits down the hall to check on Chip.

In a moment, she returns and begins to help Wade. In her travels she notices the ashtray is missing. Wade sees her searching for it but says nothing.

LYNNETTE *finds a piece of the ashtray and picks it up. She looks at it, then around at the devastated room.)*

LYNNETTE. When your father gets home, he is going to crap a fucking cupcake.

WADE. It's 'fuck*in*'. You don't pronounce the *g*.

(Lights very slowly fade as mother and son work in silence, restoring their showpiece living room to order.)

THE END

COSTUME PLOT

FEMALES

ACT ONE, SCENE ONE

LYNNETTE
Wrap Dress, ie Diane Von Furstenburg
Stylish Heels
Earrings
Necklace
Wedding Band
Engagement Ring
(Special Makeup: One eyebrow drawn w/pencil, one eyebrow bald; actress applies second eyebrow onstage)

ACT ONE, SCENE TWO

TAMMY
Halter top or Peasant Blouse
Bell-bottom jeans, slight flare
Clogs
Thin leather lace necklance w/beads

ACT TWO

TAMMY (First entrance) Same

TAMMY (Second entrance) Panties only.
Quickly puts on Wade's T-shirt.

(Author's note: The brief partial nudity in this scene serves as an ironic contrast to the playful make-out scene of the first act, and underscores Tammy's fear of Chip. The actress can cover herself with an arm, and quickly put on Wade's T-shirt facing upstage. The moment shows Tammy at her most innocent and vulnerable. Toplessness is much preferred. Tammy in 1978 would not wear a bra. That said, a bra would be an option if there are absolute objections to nudity. If a bra is used, it should be one that earthy Tammy might be convinced to wear. It should not be a lacy, frilly affair.)

LYNNETTE
Same

MALES

ACT ONE, SCENE ONE

WADE
Shorts with pockets
T-shirt, plain or with '70s logo such as Star Wars

CHIP (First entrance)
Bell-bottom Jeans (slight flare)
(Makeup special: Hair wet)

CHIP (Second entrance)
Jeans
Disco-style, tight silk shirt
Leather belt
Platform shoes

ACT ONE, SCENE TWO

WADE
Same

CHIP
Same

ACT TWO

WADE
Same
Removes T-shirt at Tammy's second entrance.

CHIP
Same Jeans.
Same Platform shoes.

FURNITURE

Living Room:
1970s stylish, pristine sofa
Matching chair
coffee table
entertainment center w/stereo
potted tropical plant
end table
lamp
decorative waste basket

Raised Foyer:
small table
vanity mirror
cuckoo clock

PROPS

ACT ONE, Scene One

Onstage:
carpet rake (tucked in a corner)
many albums (in stereo unit)
faux folk album cover & sleeve
stereo headphones
telephone (on end table)
coasters (on coffee table)
large ashtray (on coffee table; rigged to break)

Off S.L.
purse w/make-up supplies & money (Lynnette enters carrying it)
eyebrow pencil
bowl of Froot Loops

Off U.S.C.
Towel

ACT ONE, Scene Two

Onstage:
paperback E.M. Forster's A Passage To India
spiral note pad
pen
Heart's Dreamboat Annie album (in stereo unit)
Joni Mitchell's Court and Spark album (in stereo unit)

In Tammy's Jeans pocket:
cigarettes
lighter

baggie of weed
rolling papers

Off U.S.C.
Burger King pants (dark brown polyester)
wallet (in pants pocket)
twenty-two dollars (in wallet)

Off S.L.
(2) tall glasses of Seven-Up on ice
air freshener spray
vacuum cleaner

In Chip's Jeans:
baggie of white powder
small straw

ACT TWO

Onstage:
bucket w/soapy water
rag
spray water bottle
carpet rake (Wade takes it out of hidden corner)

Off U.S.C.
dumbbells
pillow case crammed with clothes
bundle wrapped in a blanket
small stereo
tissue
gauze
adhesive tape
bottle of alcohol
a few ten dollar bills

In Chip's Jeans:
car keys

SPECIAL MAKE-UP EFFECTS
Lynnette has one eyebrow missing, Act One
Chip's arm is cut and drips blood, Act Two

SPECIAL SOUND EFFECTS
Brief folky instrumental
Brief hard rock instrumental music
Radio DJ recorded speech
French lesson tape
Cuckoo clock, various cues as specified

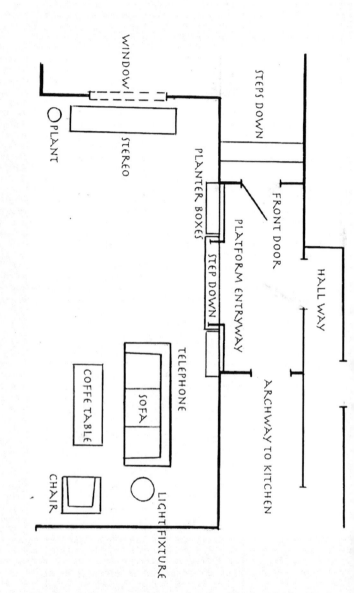

THE SUNKEN LIVING ROOM

SET DESIGN BY JESSE DREIKOSEN

WINDOW

STEREO

PLANT

PLANTER BOXES

STEP DOWN

PLATFORM ENTRYWAY

STEPS DOWN

FRONT DOOR

HALLWAY

ARCHWAY TO KITCHEN

COFFE TABLE

SOFA

TELEPHONE

CHAIR

LIGHT FIXTURE

From the Reviews of
THE SUNKEN LIVING ROOM...

"...unsettling, funny, poignant... Caudle's writing is full of humor, compassion, keen observation and period-perfect language..."
- Christine Dolen, *The Miami Herald*

"...sharp period piece... blistering family drama... The Sunken Living Room is a drama with much to say about growing up too soon in a world that's moving too fast."
- Jack Zink, *Sun Sentinel*

"Sidelined by the hurricanes, The Sunken Living Room is back at home in Miami, all the better for South Florida audiences, who get to be the first of what will surely be many audiences to experience this delicious drama."
- Mary Damiano, *Miami ArtZine*

"David Caudle's new play... is a rarity: a realistic, linear comedy-drama that holds and entertains its audience with an authentic slice of dysfunctional family life. ...funny, touching and disturbing, ...dramatically buoyant theatre."
- David Cuthbert, *Times-Picayune*

"David Caudle's masterful use of ordinary language is both colloquial and precise. He creates compelling cadences in an emotionally charged atmosphere where anger and affection, entrapment and compassion play at the edges of each utterance."
- Richard Matthews, Director, University of Tampa Press, Editor of *The Tampa Review*

Also by
David Caudle...

Feet of Clay

Please visit our website **samuelfrench.com** for complete
descriptions and licensing information

OFF-OFF-BROADWAY FESTIVAL PLAYS

TWENTY-SECOND SERIES

Brothers   This Is How It Is   Because I Wanted to Say Tremulous   The Last Dance   For Tiger Lilies Out of Season   The Most Perfect Day

TWENTY-THIRD SERIES

The Way to Miami   Harriet Tubman Visits a Therapist   Meridan, Mississippi   Studio Portrait   It's Okay, Honey   Francis Brick Needs No Introduction

TWENTY-FOURTH SERIES

The Last Cigarette   Flight of Fancy   Physical Therapy   Nothing in the World Like It   The Price You Pay   Pearls Ophelia   A Significant Betrayal

TWENTY-FIFTH SERIES

Strawberry Fields   Sin Inch Adjustable   Evening Education   Hot Rot   A Pink Cadillac Nightmare   East of the Sun and West of the Moon

TWENTY-SIXTH SERIES

Tickets, Please!   Someplace Warm   The Test   A Closer Look   A Peace Replaced   Three Tables

TWENTY-SEVENTH SERIES

Born to Be Blue   The Parrot   Flights   A Doctor's Visit   Three Questions   The Devil's Parole

TWENTY-EIGHTH SERIES

Along for the Ride   A Low-Lying Fog   Blueberry Waltz   The Ferry   Leaving Tangier   Quick & Dirty (A Subway Fantasy)

TWENTY-NINTH SERIES

All in Little Pieces   The Casseroles of Far Rockaway   Feet of Clay   The King and the Condemned   My Wife's Coat   The Theodore Roosevelt Rotunda

THIRTIETH SERIES

Defacing Michael Jackson   The Ex   Kerry and Angie   Outside the Box   Picture Perfect   The Sweet Room

THIRTY-FIRST SERIES

Le Supermarché   Libretto   Play #3   Sick   Pischer   Relationtrip

THIRTY-SECOND SERIES

Opening   Circuit Breakers   Bright. Apple. Crush   The Roosevelt Cousins, Thoroughly Sauced   Every Man   The Good Book

SAMUELFRENCH.COM

Printed in the United States
204900BV00003B/481-582/P